Mary Hill Project

Fatima Khalid

Categorie(s): Fiction, Science Fiction, Short Stories

1

"Mr. Hudson of—ah—Mastodonia," remarked the chief of protocol.

The secretary of state extended his hand to the audience. "Mr. Hudson, it's great to see you. As far as I can tell, you've been here multiple times."

"You're right," Hudson responded. "It was difficult for me to persuade your people that I was sincere."

"And, Mr. Hudson, how are you?"

"Believe me, sir, I would never attempt to deceive you."

"And this Mastodonia," the secretary said as she tapped the document on the desk. "Excuse me, but I'm not familiar with it."

""It's a new country," Hudson remarked, "but it's perfectly genuine." We have a constitution, a democratic government, duly elected politicians, and a legal system. We are a free, peace-loving people who have access to abundant natural resources and—" "

"Please tell me, sir," the secretary interjected, "just where are you located?"

"You are technically our closest neighbours."

Protocol exclaimed, "But that is ludicrous!"

"Not at all," Hudson insisted. "Mr. Secretary, if you will allow me a moment, I have substantial evidence."

He brushed the Protocol fingers from his sleeve and walked up to the desk, placing down the portfolio he was carrying.

The secretary said, "Go ahead, Mr. Hudson." "How about we all take a seat and relax while we talk things over?"

"I see you have my credentials. Here's something to think about—"

"I have a document signed by a Mr. Wesley Adams," says the narrator.

"He's our first president," Hudson explained. "You could call him our George Washington."

"Mr. Hudson, what is the objective of your visit?"

"We'd like to start diplomatic ties with you. We believe it would be beneficial to both of us. After all, we are a sister nation that shares your policies and objectives. We'd like to establish trade deals and would appreciate some assistance from Point Four." "

The secretary gave a kind smile. "Naturally. Who doesn't like it?"

Hudson said stiffly, "We're willing to contribute something in return." "For one thing, we could provide refuge."

"Sanctuary!"

"I recognise that in the current condition of international relations, a foolproof sanctuary is not something to be sniffed at," Hudson added.

The secretary became ice-cold. "I'm a really busy person."

Hudson was firmly grasped by Protocol's arm. "You're free to go."

General Leslie Bowers dialled the State Department and obtained the secretary.

""I'm sorry to trouble you, Herb," he explained, "but there's something I need to double-check." Perhaps you can assist me."

"I'm happy to assist you if I can."

"There's a guy loitering around the Pentagon, attempting to gain access to see me. He said I was the only person he'd speak to, but you know how things go." "

"I'm sure I do."

"Huston or Hudson or something along those lines."

"He was just an hour or so ago," the secretary explained. "He's a bit of a crackpot."

"Is he already gone?"

"Yes. I don't believe he'll return."

"Did he say how you could get in touch with him?"

"I don't think he did," says the narrator.

"How did he make an impression on you? What kind of impression did he leave on you?" "

"I warned you. He's a nut."

"I'm sure he is. I was concerned when he mentioned something to one of the colonels. You can't pass up anything in the Dirty Tricks Department, you know. Even if it's crazy, you have to look at it these days." "

"He promised asylum," the secretary exclaimed angrily. "Imagine that!" says the speaker.

"I believe he's been making the rounds," the general explained. "He'd gone to AEC. I told them a story about how I knew where there were massive uranium deposits. It was the AEC who informed me that he was on his way to you." "

"We get these on a regular basis. We can usually ease them out. This Hudson was slightly superior to the most of them. He came in to speak with me." "

"He said something to the colonel about having a plan that would allow us to set up hidden bases anywhere we wanted, even in enemy territory. I know what you're thinking..."

"Forget it, Les," says the narrator.

""You're probably correct," the general answered, "but this thought bothers me." Can you imagine their Iron Curtain expressions?"

The terrified little government clerk carried the portfolio to the FBI, darting suspicious glances all around him.

He informed the man who towed him, "I discovered it in a tavern down the street." "I've been going there for a long time. And I came across this portfolio at the booth. I noticed the man who must have left it there and attempted to locate him afterwards, but was unable." "

"How do you know he left it there?" says the narrator.

"I had a feeling he did. He walked out of the booth just as I walked in, and it was a little gloomy in there, so it took me a minute to notice what was laying there. Because I normally pick the same booth every day, Joe notices me coming in and brings me the usual and—" "

"Did you see this man depart the booth where you normally sit?"

"You're right."

"Then you saw the portfolio," says the narrator.

"Yes, sir," says the speaker.

"You went looking for the man, thinking it was his."

"I did exactly what you said."

"However, by the time you went looking for him, he had vanished."

"That was how it was."

"Now tell me why you brought it here in the first place. Why didn't you hand it up to management so that the man could claim it?" "

"It went something like this, sir. I had a couple of drinks and was always wondering what was in that portfolio. So I went ahead and took a look and—" "

"And it was because of what you saw that you wanted to bring it here to us."

"That's correct. I noticed—"

"Tell me nothing about what you observed. Give me your name and address, and keep quiet about it. You understand that we appreciate your consideration, but we'd prefer that you say nothing." "

"Mum's the word," the little clerk told him, her voice resonating with authority.

Dr. Ambrose Amberly, a Smithsonian palaeontologist, was contacted by the FBI.

"Doctor, we have something we'd want you to have a look at. There is a lot of cinema film."

"I'd be delighted to do so. As soon as I'm free, I'll come down. Is it possible that it will be the end of the week?"

"Doctor, this is a critical situation. The most heinous thing you've ever seen. Elephants and tigers with teeth down to their necks, big, shaggy elephants and tigers. There's a grizzly bear-sized beaver." "

"Fakes," Amberly exclaimed, annoyed. "Ingenious devices. Camera \sangles."

"That was our initial notion, but there are no gadgets or camera angles. This is the genuine article."

The palaeontologist hung up after saying, "I'm on my way."

In the smug, smartaleck gossip column, there's a snide remark: At the Pentagon, flying saucers are a thing of the past. There's another mystery that has the high brass on the edge of their seats.

2

President Wesley Adams and Secretary of State John Cooper sat glumly beneath a tree in Mastodonia's capital, waiting for the unusual envoy to return.

""I tell you, Wes," Cooper, who served as secretary of commerce, treasury, and war under several aliases, remarked, "this is a foolish thing we did." What if Chuck is unable to return? They might put him in jail, or the time unit or the chopper might be damaged. We should have just gone along with it."

"We had no choice but to stay," Adams explained. "You know what would happen if we weren't here to protect this camp and our supplies."

"That old mastodon is the only item that has caused us any problems. If he shows up again, I'm going to smack him in the brisket with a skillet." "

""That isn't the only reason, and you know it," President Adams added. We can't abandon this country now that we've built it. We must maintain control. It wouldn't be enough to just plant a flag and declare it ours. It's possible that we'll be asked to show proof of our residency. Something along the lines of the old homestead laws." "

"If something happens to that time unit or the chopper," hissed Secretary Cooper, "sure enough, we'll establish residence."

"Do you believe they'll go through with it, Johnny?"

"Who's in charge of what?"

"The United States of America. Do you believe they'll know who we are?"

"Not if they know who we are," says the narrator.

"That's what I'm concerned about."

"Chuck will persuade them to do it. He has the ability to talk a cat's skin off." "

"Sometimes I think we're approaching things in the wrong way. Chuck has the long-term perspective, which I suppose is the best. But perhaps the best thing we can do is make a quick profit and get out of here. We might rent it to a movie company or take in hunting teams for ten thousand dollars each." "

""If we can get ourselves recognised as a sovereign nation, we can accomplish all of that legally and with complete protection," Cooper assured him. No one would dare to be hostile if we negotiated a mutual defence treaty because we could squawk to Uncle Sam." "

""Everything you say is correct," Adams agreed, "but there will be questions." It isn't enough to simply stroll into Washington and be recognised. They'll be interested in learning more about us, such as our population. What if Chuck has to tell them there are three of them?" "

With a shake of his head, Cooper expressed his dissatisfaction with the situation. "Wes, he wouldn't respond that way." He'd either avoid the question or respond with diplomatic double-talk. After all, how can we be anything else? *sure* Is it true that there are only three of us? Remember, we conquered the entire continent."

"You're fully aware, Johnny, that there are no other humans in North America. The migrations from Asia can be traced back as long as 30,000 years, according to scientists. They haven't got here \syet."

Cooper pondered, "Perhaps we should have done it differently." "Perhaps we should have declared the entire world, not simply the continent, in our statement. That way, we'd be able to claim a sizable population." "

"It wouldn't have held up to the test of time. Even so, we went a bit further than was allowed by tradition. Old explorers used to stake claims to specific watersheds.

They'd pick a river and claim all of the land that the river drained. They didn't go around seizing continents." "

"That's because they never knew exactly what they had," Cooper explained. "Yes, we are. "We have the benefit of hindsight," as they say "

He leaned against the tree and gazed out over the landscape. The rolling ridges covered in enormous grazing pastures and little groves, the forest-covered, ten-mile river valley—he thought it was a lovely spot. And there were grazing herds of mastodon, gigantic bison, and wild horses everywhere, with the less gregarious species strewn around.

Old Buster, the bothersome mastodon, stood at the edge of a forest a quarter-mile away, a lone bull who had most likely been driven out of a herd by a younger rival. He had his head bowed and was curling and uncurling his trunk aimlessly as he teetered slowly, elevating one foot and then the other in a lazy-crazy manner.

Cooper reminded himself that the old cuss was lonely. That was why he hung out like a homeless dog—except he was too huge and ungainly to appeal to pets, and his temper was more than likely unstable.

Cooper noticed that the midday light was warm and that the air was the freshest he had ever smelled. Overall, it was a lovely spot, like something out of an Indian summer, perfect for a Sunday picnic or camping trip.

The breeze was just right for Mastodonia's national flag—a red rampant mastodon on a field of green—to float out from its flagstaff in front of thc tent.

""You know, Johnny," Adams continued, "there's one thing that really troubles me." We may be well off the mark if we base our assertion on precedent. The previous explorers always claimed their discoveries \sfor their nations or their ruler, never for themselves."

Cooper explained, "The premise was absolutely different." "Nobody accomplished anything for themselves back then. Everyone was always under the protection of someone else. The explorers were either funded or sponsored by their governments, and they acted under a royal charter or a patent. It's not like that with us. Ours is a privately owned company. You created the time unit from scratch. We all pitched in to help buy the helicopter. We've covered all of our costs with our own money. We never received a penny from anyone. What we discovered belongs to us."

"I hope you're right," Adams responded uncomfortably.

Old Buster had emerged from the grove and was cautiously approaching the camp. Adams took up the rifle that had been strewn across his knees.

"Wait," Cooper ordered sternly. "Perhaps he's simply bluffing. It'd be a pity to plaster him; he's such a sweet old man." "

The firearm was half-raised by Adams.

He stated, "I'll give him three more steps." "I've had it with him."

A rumble erupted from the air just above their heads. Both of them leapt to their feet.

"It's Chuck!" exclaims the narrator. Cooper screamed. "He's back!" exclaims the narrator.

The helicopter did a half-turn around the camp and landed quickly.

Old Buster was a shrinking dot far down the grassy ridge, trumpeting with horror.

3

To keep the animals out, they set nightly flames encircling the camp.

"Cutting all this wood will be the death of me yet," Adams grumbled.

Cooper stated, "We have to get to work on that stockade." "We've been fooling about for far too long. A herd of mastodon will come crashing in here some night, fire or no fire, and if they ever strike the chopper, we'll be dead ducks. It wouldn't take more than five seconds to convert us into Pleistocene Robinson Crusoes." "

"Well, now that this recognition thing has passed us by," Adams observed, "maybe we can go down to business."

""The problem is," Cooper explained, "we used up almost all of our money on the chain saw to cut this wood and Chuck's trip to Washington." A tractor is required to construct a stockade. If we tried to rassle that many logs by hand, we'd kill ourselves." "

"Perhaps we'll be able to catch some of those horses galloping around out there."

"Have you ever broken a horse?" says the narrator.

"No, that's not something I've ever attempted."

"Neither do I. Chuck, how about you?"

"Not me," the ex-ambassador stated emphatically.

Cooper squatted next to the cooking fire's coals and turned the spit. Three grouse and a half-dozen quail were on the spit. A nose-tingling aroma emanated from the massive coffee pot. In the reflector, biscuits were baking.

""We've been here for six weeks and are still living in a tent and cooking over an open fire," he explained. We'd best get busy and accomplish something." "

"First, the stockade," Adams explained, "and that needs a tractor."

"We might be able to use the helicopter."

"Are you willing to take a chance? That's where we're going. "Once something happens to it...," says the narrator "

Cooper confessed, gulping, "I guess not."

"Right now, we could use some of that Point Four assistance," Adams observed.

"They kicked me out," Hudson explained. "Everywhere I went, they eventually got around to evicting me. They were quite well-prepared." "

"Well, we gave it our best shot," Adams replied.

"And to top it off," added Hudson, "I had to go and lose all that film and now we'll have to waste our time taking more of it. "I'm not going to let another saber-tooth get so near to me while I'm holding the camera." "

"You have nothing to be concerned about," Adams countered. "With the rifle, Johnny was close behind you."

"When he released go, the muzzle was approximately a foot from my head."

Cooper demanded, "Didn't I stop him?"

"He's got his head in my lap."

"Perhaps we won't need to take any more photos," Adams speculated.

Cooper answered, "We'll have to." "There are hunters up front who would gladly pay ten thousand dollars for two weeks of hunting here. But we'd have to show them movies before we could persuade them. That scenario with the saber-toothed catapult would seal the deal."

Hudson pointed out, "If it didn't scare them away." "The inside of his throat was visible for the last several feet."

Hudson, the ex-ambassador, appeared dissatisfied. "The entire situation bothers me. The news will undoubtedly leak as soon as we bring someone in. And once news gets out, there will be men waiting for us—possibly even nations—scheming to steal the technology, either legally or forcibly. That's the thing about the films I've lost that scares me the most. Someone will discover them and figure out what's going on, but I'm hoping they won't believe it or won't be able to track us down." "

Cooper added, "We could swear the hunting groups to secrecy."

"How could a sportsman stand still in front of a mounted saber-tooth tiger or a record piece of ivory?" The same could be said for anybody we approached. A university could garner funds to send a team of scientists back here, and a film studio would pay a lot of money to utilise this spot as the setting for a caveman epic. But none of that would matter to them if they couldn't tell anyone about it.

"We'd have been set if we'd been able to gain recognised as a nation. We would be able to create and enforce our own laws and regulations. We could settle the area and establish trade. Our natural resources could be exploited. Everything would be legal and transparent. We were able to communicate who we were, where we were, and what we had to offer." "

"We haven't been licked yet," Adams explained. "We have a lot of options. Those ginseng-covered river hills are a sight to behold. Each of us can excavate a dozen pounds per day. In the root, there's a lot of money."

""Ginseng root is peanuts," Cooper explained. We require em>large/em> funds." "

"Or we could trap," Adams suggested. "There's a lot of beaver in this place."

"Have you given them beaver a good look? They're almost the same size as a St. Bernard." "

"That's even better. Consider the value of a single pelt."

"It was impossible for a dealer to believe it was beaver. He'd assume you were attempting to deceive him. There are only a few states where beaver trapping is legal. Even if you could sell the pelts, you'd have to get permits in each of those states." "

"Those mastodons have a lot of ivory," Cooper explained. "And if we wanted to proceed further north, we'd find mammoths carrying even more... "

"And get thrown in the jug for importing ivory?"

They sat there, all three of them, staring at the fire, speechless.

A large hunting cat's wailing complaint could be heard somewhere up the river.

4

Hudson was lying in his sleeping bag, peering up at the night sky. It disturbed him a great deal. There wasn't a single recognised constellation or star that he could confidently name. This fiddling of the stars, he thought, highlighted in this ancient continent more than anything else the wide chasm of years that separated him from the Earth where he had been—or would be—born.

Adams had stated that it would take a hundred and fifty thousand years, give or take ten thousand years. There was simply no way of knowing. It's possible that there will be in the future. One method could be to measure the stars and compare them to their locations in the twentieth century. However, any figure at this time could only be a guess.

The time machine couldn't be calibrated or tested to see how well it worked. In fact, there was no means to verify it em>there was/em>. He recalled that the first time they used it, they weren't sure if it would actually work. There had been no way to discover the truth. You knew it worked when it worked. And there would have been no way of knowing whether it wouldn't have worked if it hadn't.

Of course, Adams was certain, but only because he had complete faith in the half-mathematical, half-philosophic notions he had developed—concepts that neither Hudson nor Cooper could comprehend.

That had always been the case, even when they were children, with Wes concocting the schemes that he and Johnny carried out. They had also utilised time travel in their play at the time. They'd built a time machine out of a fantastic collection of salvaged trash in Johnny's back yard—a wooden crate, an empty five-gallon paint pail, a damaged coffee maker, a lot of abandoned copper tubing, a busted steering wheel, and other miscellaneous items. They had "travelled" back to Indian-before-the-white-man land, mammoth-land, and dinosaur-land in it, and the carnage had been gloriously awful, he remembered.

In actuality, though, everything had been quite different. There was a lot more to it than just shooting down the strange fauna that one came across.

They should have known there would be because they had discussed it frequently.

He remembered the university bull session and the little, usually quiet youngster who sat silently in the corner, a law-school student with the surname Pritchard.

And after a long period of silence, this Pritchard kid spoke up: " "If you ever go back in time, you'll find yourself up against a lot more than you bargained for. I'm not talking about the weather, the terrain, or the fauna; I'm talking about economics and politics." "

Hudson remembered them all jeering at him before continuing on with their conversation. After a short while, the conversation shifted to women, as it always did.

He was curious as to where that calm man was. I'll have to look him up and tell him he was correct someday, Hudson told himself.

We made a mistake, he realised. There were so many other options, but we'd been so certain and greedy—hungry for the victory and the glory—that there was no easy way to collect now.

They could have sought aid from a huge industrial organisation, an educational foundation, or even the government if they were on the edge of success. They may have gotten funding and support the same way past explorers did. They would have had protection and funding to do a proper job, and they would not have had to operate on a shoestring budget of one battered chopper and one time unit. They could have had some, if not all, rescue units on standby in the twentieth century if the need arose.

Except that would have necessitated a deal, possibly a difficult one, and sharing with someone who had provided nothing but cash. And an event like this was about more than money—it was about twenty years of hopes, a wonderful idea, and the dedication to that great vision—years of struggle, years of disappointment, and an almost fanatical reluctance to give up.

Even so, Hudson reasoned, they'd worked it out. They'd had plenty of opportunities to make mistakes, but they'd only made a handful. In the end, all they needed was some support.

Take, for example, the helicopter. It was the only way to travel across time that worked. To clear any upheavals and subsidences that had occurred throughout geologic time, you had to get up in the air. The helicopter lifted you up and kept you clear so you could choose a suitable landing spot. Traveling without it would put you in the core of a massive tree, a marsh, or the middle of a herd of frightened, violent monsters, assuming you were lucky with terrain surfaces. A plane would have sufficed, but in this universe, you couldn't land a plane—or at least, you couldn't be sure you could. However, a helicopter can land practically anyplace.

They were almost undoubtedly fortunate in terms of the time they had travelled, though it was impossible to say how much of it was luck. Wes had the impression that he wasn't working as mindlessly as he appeared to be. He had calibrated the device for 50,000-year leaps. He had admitted that finer calibration would have to wait for more development effort.

They had figured it out using the 50,000-year calibrations. One hop (if the calibration was correct) would have put them at the end of the Wisconsin glacial era; two jumps would have put them at the start. The third would place them near the conclusion of the Sangamon Interglacial, which it appears to have done—give or take ten thousand years.

They had arrived at a time when the weather did not appear to be particularly hot or chilly. The flora was contemporary enough to make them feel at ease. The contemporary and Pleistocene faunas collided. And the surface features had not changed much since the nineteenth century. The rivers followed well-worn routes, and the hills and bluffs resembled each other. At least in this part of the world, 150,000 years had made little difference.

Hudson felt boyhood dreams were fantastic. It didn't happen very often. that it may be followed by three men who had daydreamed in their youth to the very end They had, however, and now they were here.

Johnny was on the lookout, and Hudson's time was approaching, so he'd better get some rest. He closed his eyes for a moment, then opened them again to gaze at the strange stars. He noticed that the east was bathed in silver light. The Moon will rise soon, which was a wonderful thing. When the Moon was up, a man could keep a better watch.

The marrow-chilling noise that cut across the darkness grabbed him upright and into full awareness. The furious racket seemed to curdle the air, and he sat paralysed by it for a minute. Then, it appeared, his brain took the sounds and divided it into two distinct but intertwined categories: a cat's deadly shriek and a mastodon's crazed trumpeting.

The Moon had risen, and the area was bathed in its glow. Cooper, he noticed, was standing beyond the watchfires, looking around. He's keeping an eye on things, his rifle drawn. Adams was frantically trying to get out of his house. sleeping bag, gently swearing to himself The cooking fire had gone out. The building was reduced to a bed of speckled coals, yet the watchfires remained lit. were on fire, and the chopper, which had been positioned within their circle, picked them up. catching the glimmer of fire

"It's Buster," Adams snarled at him. "I'd recognise his shrieking from a mile away. Since we arrived, he's done nothing but march up and down and yell. He now appears to have gone out and procured a saber-tooth." "

Hudson zipped down his sleeping bag, grabbed his gun, and sprung to his feet, silently following Adams to Cooper's position.

Cooper made a move towards them. "Break it up as little as possible. That'll be the last time you see anything like it." "

Adams raised his rifle.

Cooper smashed the barrel with his fist.

He yelled, "You stupid!" "Do you want them to turn against us?"

The mastodon stood two hundred yards distant, with the shrieking saber-tooth on his back. The big beast leapt into the air and landed with a bang, bucking to dislodge the cat and whipping his massive trunk through the air. The cat struck and struck again with his sparkling teeth as he bucked, going for the spine.

The mastodon then slammed his head down as though doing a somersault, rolled, and landed on his feet, closer to them than he had been before. The colossal cat had escaped.

The two stood facing one other for a brief moment. Then, in the moonlight, the tiger charged, a flowing streak of motion. Buster sped away, and the cat, leaping, collided with his shoulder, scratched frantically, and slipped away. The mastodon lunged forward, tusks slicing and massive feet pounding. The cat shouted and sprang up, landing spread-eagle on Buster's head after taking a glancing hit from one of the tusks.

The elderly mastodon, enraged and terrified, and blinded by the tiger's raking claws, bolted—straight for the camp. As he ran, he grabbed the cat in his trunk and yanked him free, lifting him high and throwing him.

"Watch out!" Cooper shouted as he raised his rifle and fired.

FHudson saw everything as though it were a single scenario, frozen, one frame stolen from a spectacular movie epic—the charging mastodon, with the tiger hoisted and the sound track one big explosion of ferocious chaos.

The scene then vanished in a flurry of movement. He knew he had fired when his rifle thudded against his shoulder, but he didn't hear the boom. And the mastodon was practically on top of him, tearing into him like some huge and ruthless destroyer.

The huge brushed by him as he hurled himself to one side. He watched the hurled saber-tooth drop to Earth within the circle of the watchfires out of the corner of his eye.

He raised his weapon and focused his sights on the area behind Buster's ear. He drew the gun and pulled the trigger. The mastodon staggered for a moment, then regained his footing and continued on his way. He went straight through one of the watchfires, scattering coals and flaming brands.

Then there was a thump and a metallic shrieking clang.

"Oh no!" exclaimed Hudson.

They rushed ahead and came to a halt inside the circle of fires.

The helicopter was teetering on the edge of a cliff. One of the rotor blades was bent. The mastodon was half-way across it, as though he had stumbled as he tried to bulldoze his way through it.

Something crawled towards them, its spitting, snarling lips gaping in the firelight, its back broken, rear legs dragging.

Adams calmly and silently fired a bullet into the saber-head. tooth's

5

General Leslie Bowers got out of his chair and took a brisk walk around the room. He came to a halt and slammed his fist into the conference table.

He sobbed at them, "You can't do it." "You're not going to be able to terminate the project." I *know* There's a glimmer of truth in that. We're not going to give up!"

"But, General, it's been ten years," remarked the army secretary. "They'd be here by now if they were coming back."

The general's pacing came to a halt as he stiffened. Who did that little civilian squirt think he was, speaking to the military in such a tone?

"We understand how you feel, General," the chairman of the Joint Chiefs of Staff remarked. "I believe we're all aware of how deeply you're connected. You've been blaming yourself for years when you don't have to. After all, it's possible that there's nothing to it."

"Sir," the general said. *know* There's a glimmer of truth in that. Even when no one else did, I believed it at the time. And everything we've discovered since confirms my suspicions. Let's take a closer look at these three gentlemen. We didn't know much about them at the time, but we do now. I've followed their lives from the time they were born till they vanished—and, just in case it's all a scam, we've looked for them for years and found nothing.

"I spoke with people who knew them and looked into their academic and service records. I've come to the conclusion that if any three men were capable of doing it, they were the ones. Adams was the brains behind the operation, while the other two followed out his plans. Cooper was a bulldog who could keep them going, while Hudson was the one who would find out the angles.

"And, gentlemen, they were aware of the angles." They'd doped everything up.

"What Hudson tried in Washington is a good example of that." They were thinking about those aspects while in school. I spoke with Pritchard, a New York lawyer, a few years ago. He informed me that they talked about the economic and political challenges they would face if they ever figured out what they were working on back in university.

"Wesley Adams was one of our most promising young scientists. That is supported by his academic record as well as his military service. There were at least a dozen careers he could have taken after the war. He, on the other hand, was uninterested. And I'll explain why he wasn't there. He had a broader project in mind, one he wanted to concentrate on. So he and the other two went off on their own—" "

The army secretary cut in, "You suppose he was working on a temporal—"

The general screamed, "He was working on a time machine!" "I'm not sure about this 'temporal' thing. For me, the term 'time machine' is sufficient." "

"Let's cool down, General," the JCS chairman responded, "there's no need to yell."

The general gave a nod. "Sir, please accept my apologies. This gets me all heated up. I've been dealing with it for the past ten years. I'm trying to make up for what I didn't do ten years ago, as you say. I should've approached Hudson. Sure, I was busy, but not that busy. It's an official attitude that we're too busy to see anyone, and I admit that I'm guilty of it. And now that you're bringing the endeavour to a close—" "

The army secretary stated, "It's costing us money."

"And we have no direct evidence," the JCS chairman pointed out.

"I have no idea what you're talking about," the general snarled. "Wesley Adams was the only guy living who could break the rules of time. We discovered his workplace. We identified the workshop and spoke with neighbours who stated something strange was going on and—" "

"But ten years, General!" exclaimed the army secretary.

"We kicked Hudson out after he brought us the greatest discovery in human history. Do you think they'll come crawling back to us after that?" "

"Do you believe they went somewhere else?"

"That's not something they'd do. They understand the significance of what they've discovered. They were not going to sell us out."

The man from the state agency remarked, "Hudson arrived with a ludicrous idea."

The general roared, "They had to defend themselves!" "What would you do if you discovered a virgin planet with all of its natural resources intact? Come on down and hand it over to a government that is too 'busy' to notice—" "

"General!"

"Yes, sir," the fatigued general apologised. "I wish you gentlemen could see how it all comes together in my opinion." Then there were the films, and we have a dozen skilled palaeontologists on our side who say it's impossible to manufacture something as perfect as those. Even if they were, there are some disparities that no one would ever consider faking because no one would ever know. Who, for example, would place lynx tassels on a saber-ears? tooth's Who'd have guessed a young mastodon was black?

"And then there's the place. I'm wondering whether you've forgotten that it was because to those films that we were able to trace down the site of Adams' workshop. They provided us such strong leads that we didn't even think twice about driving directly to the abandoned farm where Adams and his friends had worked. Don't you see how everything connects?"

"I assume you have an explanation as to why they chose that particular site," the state department official remarked angrily.

"You thought you had me there," the general continued, "but I've got a solution for you." It's a good one. Wisconsin's southwestern corner is a geologic anomaly. All of the glaciations had missed it. We have no idea why. Whatever the reason, the glaciers encroached on both sides and far to the south of it, leaving it as a small island in a sea of ice.

"Also, except for a brief period during the Triassic, that same part of Wisconsin has always been dry ground. That, along with a few other places, are the only places in North America that have not been repeatedly flooded. I don't think it's necessary to emphasise how comforting it would be for an experimental time traveller to know that he'd have dry soil beneath him in practically every age he would encounter." "

"We've given this topic a lot of consideration and, while we don't feel competent to decide on the probability or impossibility of time travel, there are certain remarks I'd like to make at some point," the economist said.

"Go ahead and do it right now," the JCS chairman urged.

"We only have one complaint to the whole thing. Naturally, one of the reasons we were interested in it was that, if true, it would provide us with an entirely new planet to exploit, possibly more intelligently than we have in the past. However, it comes to me that any planet has a finite quantity of natural resources. What effect would going back in time and exploiting those resources have on what is left of those resources for use in the present? Wouldn't we be robbing ourselves of our own heritage if we did this?" "

""That assertion would not hold true in every circumstance," the AEC chairman remarked. In fact, the opposite is true. We know that there was a lot more uranium in the past than there is currently in various geologic epochs. You could catch the uranium before it transformed into lead if you went back far enough. There is a lot of lead in southwestern Wisconsin. We assumed Hudson was a madman talking through his hat when he said he knew the location of large uranium resources. We would have picked him up right away if we had known—be let's honest—if we had known and believed him about going back in time, none of this would have occurred." "

"It wouldn't hold true in forests, either," the JCS chairman stated. "Or with meadows or crops," says the narrator.

The economist looked a little flushed. "There's something else," he explained. "What would happen if we went back in time and colonised the area we found? What would happen when that retroactive civilization reaches the beginning of our historic period? What will be the outcome of this cultural clash? Will the course of history be altered? Is it possible that what happened was a hoax? That's all—"

"That's all nonsense!" exclaimed the commander. "That, and this other discussion about depleting resources. Whatever we've done in the past — or are about to do — has already been done. I've been up nights, mister, contemplating all of these issues, and there is no answer, believe me, except the one I give you. The question that we are confronted with here is a pressing one. Do we give up everything or do we keep watching that Wisconsin farm for them to return? Do we continue to look for the procedure, formula, or mechanism that Adams discovered for going through time on our own?" "

"So far, General, we've had no luck in our research," replied the silent physicist at the table's far end. "If you weren't so convinced, and the proof wasn't so compelling that it had been done by Adams, I'd say it's impossible. We don't have a single strategy that offers any hope. Flounder is the greatest word to describe what we've done so far. But if Adams was able to pull it off, it must be doable. There could be more than one way to look at it. We'd like to continue our efforts."

"Not a single syllable of criticism has been thrown on you for your failure," the chairman said to the scientist. " It looks to be beyond human comprehension that you could achieve it. If Adams was the perpetrator—*if* Hc did, I say—it must simply have been that he came across a line of investigation that no one else had thought about."

""You will recall," the general replied, "that the research programme was viewed as purely a gamble from the beginning." Our only hope was, and continues to be, that they would return." "

"It would have been so much easier all around if Adams had patented his idea," the state department official stated.

The general was furious with him. "And had it published in the patent office records, all neat and organised, so that anyone who wanted it could look it up and get it?"

"We may be eternally grateful that he didn't patent it," the chairman remarked.

6

The helicopter would never take to the air again, but the time machine remained intact.

That didn't imply it was going to succeed.

At their campsite, they held a powwow. They determined that moving the camp was easier than removing the body of Old Buster. As a result, they had shifted early in the morning, leaving the old mastodon sprawled across the chopper.

The carrion birds, lesser cats, wolves and foxes, and little skulkers would cleanly pick the large bones in a day or two, they knew.

It had taken a long time to get the time unit out of the chopper, but they had eventually done so, and Adams sat with it cradled in his lap.

""The worst part is that I can't test it," he explained. There isn't any way to do it. When you switch it on, it either works or it doesn't. You won't know unless you give it a shot."

Cooper answered, "That's something we can't help with." "The issue, it seemed to me, is how we'll use it without the whirlybird."

"We have to figure out a means to get up in the air," remarked one of the team members. Adams. "We don't want to risk climbing up into the mountains. twenty-first century, and he was nearly six feet tall when he arrived. underground."

Hudson pointed out, "Common sense suggests we should be higher here than up ahead." "These hills have existed since the Jurassic period. They were undoubtedly much higher back then and have since worn down. Weathering should still be occurring. As a result, we should be higher here than we were in the twentieth century—not by much, but higher." "

Cooper inquired, "Did anyone ever notice what the altimeter read?"

Adams said, "I don't believe I did."

Hudson said, "It wouldn't inform you anyway." "It would only give us our height then and now—and remember, we were moving—and what about air pockets and relative atmospheric density and all that?"

Cooper appeared to be as disheartened as Hudson.

"How does this sound?" Adams inquired. "We'll construct a twelve-foot-high platform. That should be sufficient to clear us while remaining small enough to remain within the range of the unit's force-field." "

"What if we're two feet higher here?" says the narrator. Hudson made a point.

"Unless a man is plain unlucky, a fourteen-foot fall would not kill him."

"It has the potential to break some bones."

"As a result, it has the potential to break several bones. Do you want to risk a broken leg by staying here?" "

"If you put it that way, it's fine. You mention a platform. "A platform made of what?" says the narrator "

"Timber. There's a plenty of it. "All we have to do now is go out and cut some logs." "

"A twelve-foot log is substantial. "How are we going to get so huge a log uphill?" says the narrator "

"We're dragging it."

"You mean, we try."

"Perhaps we could put together a cart," Adams speculated after a few moment of thought.

Cooper inquired, "Out of what?"

"Perhaps roller skates. "We could chop some and roll the logs up here," says the narrator "

"On flat terrain, that might work," Hudson added. "It's impossible to roll a log uphill. It was going to get away from us. "Someone could be killed." "

Cooper said, "The logs would have to be longer than twelve feet anyway." "You'd have to bury them, which would take away some video."

"Why not use the tripod principle?" says the narrator. Hudson made an offer. "Raise three logs by securing them at the top."

"A gin-pole, or primitive derrick, is what that is. It would still need to be more than twelve feet long. Maybe fifteen or sixteen years old. How are we going to get three sixteen-foot logs into the truck? We'd need a tackle and a block." "

"There's something else," Cooper added. "A portion of those logs may be beyond the force-effective field's range." A portion of them would be required to—*need to*, Mind you, portion couldn't move in time. That would cause a lot of worry... "

""Another issue is that we'd travel with the logs," Hudson remarked. I don't want to emerge from another period with a swarm of logs buzzing around me." "

"Keep your spirits up," Adams advised. "Perhaps the device won't work in the first place."

7

In his office, the general sat alone, his head between his hands. The knuckleheads, he thought, the goddamned knuckleheads! Why were they unable to see it as plainly as he did?

He'd been living with it for fifteen years as the head of Project Mastodon, and he could see all the possibilities as plainly as if they were real. Not just military options, though being a military man, he would naturally consider them first.

For example, hidden bases can be found within the fortresses of possible enemies—within, yet centuries apart in time. Many centuries apart but only a few seconds apart.

He could see it all: the fleets materialising; the sudden, devastating blow; and the instantaneous retreat into the past's fastnesses. Terrible destruction, yet no ships or people were lost.

Except that if you've got the bases, you'll never need to hit the batter. There would never be a provocation if you had the bases and let the adversary know you had them.

On the domestic front, there would be effective air-raid shelters. You'd evacuate your populace through time rather than space. You'd be safe from any form of bombing, whether it was fission, fusion, bacteriological, or whatever else the labs had on hand.

And if the worst happened—which it never would with that setup—you'd have a safe haven where the entire country could go, leaving the enemy to scavenge the empty, blown citics and lcthally powdery countryside.

Hudson had given sanctuary to the then-secretary of state fifteen years before, and the imbecile had frozen up at the insult and had Hudson booted out.

Consider the living space and the immense new chances that would arise if war did not occur—not the least of which would be the possibility to attain peaceful living in a virgin planet, where old hatreds would slough off and new concepts would have a chance to bloom.

He was curious about the whereabouts of the three people who had travelled through time. Maybe he's dead. A mastodon has trampled you. Alternatively, you could be pursued by tigers. Or perhaps they were killed by warlike tribesmen. He kept forgetting that there weren't any at the time. Alternatively, you could be trapped in time, unable to return, and sentenced to exile in an alternate universe. Or maybe he was just plain disgusted, he reasoned. And if they were, he couldn't blame them.

Or, let's be imaginative, smuggling in colonists from somewhere other than the closely guarded Wisconsin farm and establishing the nation they claimed to be.

They needed to return to the present as soon as possible, or Project Mastodon would perish. The study programme had already been terminated, and if nothing was done fast, the watch that had been established on the Wisconsin farm would be lifted.

"And if they do that," the general said, "I know exactly what I'm going to do."

He stood up and took a brisk walk around the room.

"By God, I'll show 'em!" he exclaimed.

8

The pyramid had taken ten days of backbreaking labour to construct. They'd dragged the rocks from a stream bed half a mile away and piled them stone by stone to a full twelve feet in height. It needed a lot of rocks and a lot of patience, because the pyramid's base naturally broadened out as it rose.

But now everything was in place.

Hudson sat in front of the smouldering flame, blistering hands in front of him.

It should function better than the logs and be less risky, he reasoned.

Take a fistful of sand in your hand. Some of it trickled back between your fingers, but the most of it stayed in your grip. That was the underlying principle of the stone pyramid. Most of the rocks would go along with the time machine if it ever worked.

Those who refused to leave would simply trickle out and cause no harm. There would be no stress or strain to disrupt the force-operation. field's

What happens if the time unit doesn't work?

Or, if it did, how did you know?

No matter how you looked at it, this was the end of the dream, Hudson thought.

Even if they returned to the twentieth century, they would have no money, and with the film lost and no replacement taken, they would have no proof that they had been back beyond the birth of history—almost to the dawn of Man.

Although it would make no difference how far you travelled. It would be the same if you could span an hour or a million years; if you could span an hour, you could span a million years. And if you could go back a million years, you could go back to the first tick of eternity, the first stir of time across the face of emptiness and nothingness—back to that first instant when nothing had happened, nothing had been planned, nothing had been thought, when the entire Universe was a blank slate waiting for the first chalk stroke of destiny.

Another helicopter would cost $30,000, and they didn't have enough money to buy the tractor they needed to construct the stockade.

Borrowing was not an option. You couldn't walk into a bank and tell them you needed $30,000 to travel back to the Stone Age.

You might still approach an industry, a university, or the government, and if you could persuade them that you were on to something, they might put up the money after taking a cut of almost all of the earnings. And, of course, they'd run the show because it was their money, and all you'd done was sweat and blood.

Cooper broke the stillness by saying, "There's one thing that still worries me." "We spent a lot of time scouting locations so we wouldn't miss the barn and home, as well as all the other structures..."

"Don't tell me about the windmill!" says the narrator. Hudson was in tears.

"No. I believe we've cleared it up. But, as far as I can tell, we're right up against that barbed-wire fence at the orchard's south end." "

"We could relocate the pyramid over twenty feet or so if you like."

Cooper sighed. "With the fence, I'll take a chance." With the time unit tucked beneath his arm, Adams rose to his feet. "Come on, you knuckleheads. It's time for me to leave."

They cautiously ascended the pyramid and stood unsteadily at the summit.

Adams shifted the unit to his chest and clutched it.

""Stand close together and bend your knees a little," he said. It might be a big decrease." "

"Go ahead," Cooper said. "Turn on the switch."
The button was pressed by Adams.
There was no action.
The device was not functional.

9

When he finished speaking, the director of Central Intelligence remained silent.

"Are you certain of your facts?" the President inquired.

"In my whole life, Mr. President," the CIA director said, "I've never been more certain of anything."

With a question in his eyes, the President looked to the other two people in the room.

"It checks, sir, with everything we know," the JCS chairman stated.

"However, it's incredible!" exclaimed the President.

"They're terrified," the CIA director remarked. "They spend their evenings awake. They've come to believe that we're about to journey across time. They've tried and failed before, but they believe we're on the verge of success. They believe that if they don't hit us now, they won't be able to hit us later, since once we obtain time travel, they'll realise they've been outnumbered." "

"However, we abandoned Project Mastodon over three years ago. It's been ten years since we put the research on hold. It's been twenty-five years since Hudson—" "

"That doesn't make a difference, sir. They believe we dropped the project publicly but took it underground. That's the kind of technique they'd be able to comprehend." "

The President took out a pencil and began scribbling on a paper.

""Who was the old general who made such a fuss when we dropped the project?" he wondered. I recall being in the Senate at the time. He came over to talk to me."

"Bowers, sir," said the chairman of the JCS.

"That's correct. What happened to him?"

"Retired."

"Well, I suppose it makes no difference now." He doodled some more before saying, " "This, gentlemen, appears to be the end. How long did you say we'd have?"

"Sir, not more than ninety days. It's possible that it'll be as little as thirty."

The President raised his eyes to the head of the JCS.

""We're as ready as we'll ever be," stated the chairman. We should be able to handle them, I believe. Of sure, there will be some—"

"I understand," the President admitted.

"Could we bluff?" the secretary of state wondered softly. "I'm sure it wouldn't stick, but it'll buy us some time."

"Do you mean you're implying we have timc travel?"

The secretary smiled and nodded.

"It wouldn't work," the CIA director grumbled. "There would be no doubt if we truly had it. If they were convinced we had it, they'd become extraordinarily well-mannered, almost neighbourly." "

"But we don't have it," the President lamented.

10

With a deer strung on a pole they carried on their shoulders, the two hunters trekked home late in the day. As they strolled along, their breath hung noticeably in the air, for the frost had arrived, and they knew there would be snow any day now.

"I'm concerned about Wes," Cooper remarked, his breathing heavy. "He's taking it way too seriously. We must keep a close check on him."

"Let's take a break," Hudson grumbled.

They came to a halt and began lowering the deer to the ground.

"He puts too much guilt on himself," Cooper added. He wiped the sweat from his brow. "There's no reason to. We all came into it with our eyes wide open." "

"He knows he's lying to himself, but it offers him something to work with. He'll be fine as long as he can keep himself occupied with his tinkering." "

"Chuck, he's not going to fix the timepiece."

"I'm sure he isn't. And he's well aware of it. He lacks the necessary tools and materials. He might have a chance back at the workshop, but not here." "

"He's having a hard time."

"It's been difficult for all of us."

"We didn't receive a notion that stranded two old friends in the middle of nowhere, though. And no matter how much we tell him that it's fine, we can't get him to swallow it." "

"Wow, Johnny, that's a lot to take in."

"How are we going to get out of this, Chuck?"

"We've found a location to call home, and there's plenty to eat. Save our ammo for the larger game—each bullet will eat a lot of food—and catch the lesser animals." "

"I'm curious as to what will happen when the flour and other supplies are depleted. We don't have a lot of money since we always thought we'd be able to get more." "

"We'll survive on beef," Hudson added. "We had millions of bison. The Plains Indians were the only ones who lived on them. We'll find roots in the spring and berries in the summer. We'll also harvest a half-dozen different kinds of nuts in the fall." "

"No matter how careful we are with it, our ammo will run out at some point."

"Bows and arrows are a type of weapon used in archery. Slingshots. Spears."

"There are a lot of monsters here that I wouldn't want to face with just a spear."

"We're not going to stand up to them. When we can, we'll duck; when we can't, we'll flee. We're no kings of creation without our guns—at least not in this area. We'll have to accept the fact if we want to live." "

"And if one of us becomes sick, or if one of us breaks a leg, or—"

"We'll give it our all. Nobody lives indefinitely."

But, Hudson realised, they were talking around the thing that concerned them the most—each of them frightened to utter the thought aloud.

So far as food, shelter, and clothing were concerned, they'd be OK. And they'd live comfortably most of the time, because this was a fat and generous land where a man might easily make a living.

But the real issue—the one they were reluctant to discuss—was their sense of purposelessness. They needed to establish purpose in a world without society in order to survive.

A guy alone on a desert island may always hope, but there was none here. A Robinson Crusoe could only be removed from his fellow people by a few thousand miles at most. They were a hundred and fifty thousand years apart here.

So far, Wes Adams has been the lucky one. Even though he was playing a thousand-to-one shot, he clung to a cause, however small it was: the hope of repairing the time machine.

We don't need to keep an eye on him right now, Hudson reasoned. We'll have to keep an eye on him when he's forced to acknowledge he can't fix the machine.

There had been enough to keep Hudson and Cooper sane, what with the cabin to be built, the winter's supply of wood to be chopped, and the hunting to be done.

But eventually, all of the chores would be completed, and there would be nothing left to do.

Cooper inquired, "Are you ready to go?"

"Sure. Now that you're all rested, "Hudson remarked.

They re-started by hoisting the pole to their shoulders.

Hudson had stayed up all night thinking about it, but all of his ideas had come to a halt.

It would be meaningless to create a Pleistocene natural history, complete with images and sketches, because no future scientist would ever have the opportunity to read it.

Or they may struggle to build a memorial, perhaps a massive pyramid, that would send a message across fifteen hundred generations, grabbing for a semblance of immortality with their bare hands. However, if they did, they would be working against the understanding that it would all be for naught, because they already knew that no such pyramid existed in historic times.

Alternatively, they could set out to find modern Man by hiking across four thousand miles of wilderness to the Bering Strait and crossing into Asia. And, having discovered modern Man hiding in his caves, they may be able to assist him tremendously on his way to inheriting a vast fortune. Except they'd never make it, and even if they did, modern Man would definitely find a method to kill them, and perhaps devour them in the process.

They emerged from the bushes and saw the cabin, which was only a hundred yards away. It huddled against the hillside above the spring, the expanse of grassland behind it billowing to the slate-gray skyline. They noticed the door was open when they noticed a trickle of smoke coming up from the chimney.

"We shouldn't keep it open like that," Cooper added. "You never know when a bear will decide to pay you a visit."

Hudson yelled, "Hey, Wes!"

But he was nowhere to be seen.

A white sheet of paper sat on the table top inside the cabin. With Cooper at his shoulder, Hudson took it up and read it.

Greetings, gentlemen— I don't want to raise your expectations and then let you down. But I believe I've discovered the source of the problem. I'm going to give it a shot. If that doesn't work, I'll return and burn this message without saying anything. If you find the note, though, you'll know it worked, and I'll return to fetch you. Wes.

In his hand, Hudson crumpled the note. "What a moron!"

Cooper exclaimed, "He's gone insane." "He was just thinking..."

They both had the same thought and dashed for the door. They skidded to a halt at the cabin's corner and stood there, staring up at the ridge above them.

The granite pyramid they'd created two months before was vanished!

11

General Leslie Bowers (retired) was about two feet out of bed when the crash occurred, his ageing muscles tensed and his white beard bristling.

The commander was a man of activity even at his advanced age. After swinging his feet out to the floor and flipping aside the covers, he reached for the shotgun resting up against the wall.

He stumbled out of the bedroom, through the dining room, and stormed into the kitchen while muttering. He flipped the switch to turn on the floodlights right there, next to the door. To get to the porch, he nearly tore the door off its hinges. He then stood there with the shotgun poised and ready, his bare feet gripping the planks and his nightshirt billowing in the wind.

He shouted, "What's going on out there?"

Where he had parked his automobile, a huge mound of rocks was lying there. Out of the ruins, a headlight and a crumpled fender were visible.

A man was carefully descending the scattered stones while swerving around the damaged fender.

The general struggled to maintain composure as he pulled back the gun's hammer.

As he descended to the bottom of the heap, the man turned to face him. The general observed that he was tightly holding something to his chest.

"The commander warned him, "Mister, your justification had better be solid. That automobile was brand-new. And for the first time since my teeth stopped hurting, I was prepared for a night of sleep "

Simply standing, the man turned to face him.

The general yelled, "Who in thunder are you?

The man moved forward gently. At the base of the stoop, he came to a stop.

He said, "My name is Wesley Adams. "I'm—"

The military leader yelled, "Wesley Adams!" Where have you been for all these years, my God?

Well, I doubt you'll accept this, but the truth is...

"You have been anticipated by us. for a very long time—25 years! Or, \srather,*I've* been expecting you. The rest of those moron gave up. Since they called off the guard three years ago, I have been waiting exactly here for you, Adams.

Adams sucked in. "I apologise for the car. See, it was done in this manner "

He observed the general grinning adoringly at him.

The commander answered, "I had faith in you.

He extended an invitation by waving the shotgun. "Please enter. I need to make a call "

Adams climbed the stairs stumbling.

The general commanded, shuddering, "Move!" "On both counts! Do you want me to succumb to the cold outside? "

He looked around the interior for the lights and turned them on. He picked up the phone and spread the shotgun across the kitchen table.

He commanded, "Give me the White House in Washington." "I did indeed say the White House. A President? He is obviously the person I want to speak with. Yes, everything is fine. He won't mind if I call."

Adams answered hesitantly, "Sir."

The general raised his head. "Adam, what is it? By all means, say it "

"Did you mention *twenty-five*years?"

"What I stated was that. What did you accomplish throughout that time?"

Adams hung on by grabbing the table. However, it wasn't.

The general replied to the operator, "Yes. Yes, I'll hold off.

He questioned Adams while keeping his hand on the phone and looking at the device. "I anticipate that you'll desire the previous terms."

"Terms?"

"Sure. Recognition. Aid at Point Four. defence agreement"

"I guess so," Adams replied.

He was cheerfully informed by the general, "You got these saps across the barrel." "You can obtain whatever you desire. After everything you did and the treatment you received, you grade it as well—especially for not giving in "

12

The bulletin was read directly off the teletype by the night editor.

What do you know, he replied. Mastodonia was just recognised by us.

He turned to face the chief copy.

He questioned, "Where the hell is Mastodonia?"

Copy chief shook his head. "Never ask me. You are the brains of this operation "

The night editor remarked, "Well, let's acquire a map for the following edition.

13

The saber-toothed cat, Tabby, dipped his powerful paw amusingly at Cooper.

He was also punched in the ribs by Cooper, who was acting cheeky.

At him, Tabby hissed.

Cooper yelled, "Show your teeth at me, please." "You express your thanks for having been raised from a kitten. If you do that just once more, I'll chop you "

After delightfully falling asleep, Tabby started washing his face.

The day that cat skips a meal, said Hudson, "is the day you're done."

Cooper reassured him, "Gentle as a dove." It wouldn't harm a fly, so.

One positive aspect is that nothing dared touch us with that beast nearby.

"the ideal watchdog ever. We must have something to protect all of our possessions. We'll both be millionaires by the time Wes returns. The ivory, ginseng, and all those furs."

"*If* He comes back.

"He's coming back. Stop worrying, please."

But it's been five years, said Hudson.

"He'll return. That's all that happened: something. He's probably already engaged in it. It's possible that when he rebuilt the device, the time setting was incorrect, or Buster's collision with the helicopter may have thrown it off-balance. It would take some time to solve that. I'm not concerned that he won't return. Why did he leave us, though, is something that I'm baffled by "

Hudson said, "I've told you. He was concerned that it wouldn't work.

"There was no reason to be terrified of that. We wouldn't have made fun of him "

"No. Naturally, we wouldn't."

"So, what?" *was* he frightened of? Cooper enquired.

"Wes was worried that if the unit failed and we knew it had failed, we would try to convince him that the situation was absurd and hopeless. He was aware that we would probably persuade him, which would end any hope for him. And that, Johnny, he wanted to hold onto. Even when there was no longer any hope, he tried to cling to it "

That is irrelevant at this time, Cooper added. "The important thing is that he will return. In my bones, I can sense it."

And here's yet another instance of hope pleading for the right to continue existing, thought Hudson.

God, I wish I could be so blind, he said.

Wes is working on it right now, Cooper replied with assurance.

14

He was. Not just him, but thousands of others were labouring frantically, realising that there was not much time left, working not just for the two men caught in time, but also for the serenity of which they had always dreamed. that throughout the ages, the entire world had craved for.

For the time machines they planned to construct to be of any use, they had to be able to zero them in just like an artilleryman zeroes a battery of guns, have each one transport its users to the same point in time in the past, and have their operations last for the same amount of time, down to the exact second.

Starting with a prototype that was calibrated for leaps of 50,000 years as its finest adjustment, the issue was one of control and calibration.

Finally, Project Mastodon had begun.

www.ingramcontent.com/pod-product-compliance
Lightning Source LLC
LaVergne TN
LVHW020525160826
845677LV00015B/3900

* 9 7 9 8 8 4 8 3 6 8 1 3 0 *